Field's Gate

Aaron Lynch

Editor: Kimberly Daries

Chapter 1

No wind blew across the field as Lisa lay dazedly among the grass. The air held the cold of a winter long since gone refusing to allow the tepid weather of spring to arrive. Neither bird nor insect or cloud dared to mar the perfect light blue sky, yet, a silent hum of orchestral instruments stained the air, playing somewhere unseen. Standing, she examined the endless expanse of emerald, ankle high grass. The ground felt as ice, a welcome relief for her travel worn feet. How far had she traveled? This she couldn't answer, but she knew she had to continue on towards the horizon, towards the sounds.

Trudging forward only accentuated her loneliness. The only thing coming into view after hours, or perhaps minutes, she could never be sure with time flowing so strangely in this realm, was an incredibly tall column. It appeared simply to sprout from beneath the field, growing steadily as she drew closer, looking to scrape the sky itself. Its width was immense, consuming the horizon with every step she took, as if her movements were commanding it to do so. Despite being so massive, no detail of its surface could be determined at such distance. Lisa tried to reason what the odd shape could be, feeling she'd seen something like it in her travels, but a white haze pushed back her intrusive thoughts, restricting her from dipping even a hand into the shallows of her mind. Eventually she gave up, the throbbing being much too painful.

Closer she drew and still nothing could be said of the material this column possessed and the louder the humming became. The nature of the eerie tune remained a mystery, every sorrowful note melded together into an unrecognizable flurry of murmurs. Lisa stopped, ogling at this new and strange thing for long moments. A twinge of fear gripped at her heart. Scowling she took a deep, calming breath, ridding her of the bothersome feeling. There was no reason to feel like this! This thing was hardly dangerous, or, perhaps it was? The thought was but a dying flicker of a candle. Up until now she'd come across nothing, no animals, no trees, not even a breeze had passed in her journey and the uncountable hours blurred together, dissolving into one incredibly long day from which she couldn't escape by neither sleep or the passage of time.

Nevertheless she walked on, determined that somehow she'd reach something, anything, eventually. Now finally she had and she wasn't going to squander this moment on a bout of uneasiness.

The wall stood nearly a hundred feet high, appearing, from this angle, as if rooted not in the ground but the sky. The many branches, wide deciduous leaves and purple flowers of the hedge created such a thick veil all but a few speckles of light broke through. A gate half the height of the wall, and constructed of the finest quartz with intricate carvings of strange birds, snakes, deer, and other indistinguishable forms, underneath a canopy of shadow at the bottom, stood within its enveloping braches. Carved into its center a leviathan, with long webbed frills along its back, shrinking as they wrapped to its tail and even longer antenna, sat coiled against the rock as if it were flat ground and not hung precariously above, its head dangling with its eyes closed. A long vertical line broke through its center, though hidden once at the serpent, revealing the door to be consumed into both sides of the bramble along its border when opened.

Gasping at the spectacle, she drew closer, never having seen anything so beautiful in her life. The gate seemed to shine and sparkle in the perpetual sunlight bathing the never-ending field around her.

Though the rock was gorgeous, it had a strange brooding air about it, the leviathan in particular, as if it could hurt her by simply being in its presence. She scoffed at the ridiculous thought, reaching out uneasily to the light speckled stone. A simple carving couldn't possibly attack. She nearly placed a hand on the gate before pulling back feeling something tug at her blue dress. She spun around to catch the assailant but, unfortunately, only succeeded in startling the little creature calling her attention. It cowered low in the grass awaiting her to strike it. Crouching down to come face to face with the whimpering red fox Lisa reached out to its head. Surprisingly, it accepted her affection with great enjoyment, standing again and panting. Its breath oddly didn't smell of iron or mould, an odour common among carnivores, but instead had a pleasant scent of some indiscernible fruit and its fur held the softness comparable to a duckling.

"Well, aren't you a peculiar little girl," Lisa said, with a sombre, yet relieved smirk. She looked back to the gate then again to the fox. The little creature backed away, its ears tilting back. "It makes you uneasy, huh? That's alright... I don't like the looks of it either."

The fox backed farther away looking about to turn tail and run. Thinking perhaps her voice was startling it Lisa took a careful step towards the petrified animal before crouching down and outstretching her hand once more. This proved a mistake. It whimpered before spinning around and running.

"Wait! C-come back!" Lisa shouted forgetting her previous wonderings, but to no avail.

The last bit of red tail vanished around the colossal hedge in an instant, leaving her alone once again. She turned back to the gate, perplexed. It hadn't changed in any noticeable way, not a branch had been snapped nor flower stood out of place. Hesitantly she approached, but took not a step before freezing, held by the spectral hand of fear, real fear, on her shoulders.

The door hadn't moved, no light escaped its central split, no figure within the shadows shifted, but one thing was different. The leviathan's eyes had opened! Before she could move, it slithered down off the slab to the grass leaving a swirling divot in the quartz behind. It vanished beneath the sea of emerald before encircled its speckled body around her, trapping her like a pig for slaughter within a pen of scales. It coiled its remaining length before her leaving it to look the part of a massive pile of discoloured, web-frilled rope adorned with a head. It flexed the fish-like fins behind its eyes and underneath its chin and its antenna flowed like a gentle stream from its nose tip at every breath. Raising its head, it glared at Lisa with solid black eyes.

"W-what are you?" Lisa asked, unable to think of anything else.

She could try to run, but the thing would pick her off in a single strike before she got one hand past its serrated spines. Despite the hopelessness of escape, she chanced one instinctive step backward. The creature pushed her towards its head with the tip of its tail, and she made no further arguments to its suggestion.

"I am the one that guards this gate," it said, its deep voice trailing off with a sombre hiss.

Lisa looked to the gate again hearing a rise in the murmurs of music within.

4

"C-can... can you tell me what this place is?" the words came out as a bullfrog's croak through her constricted throat forcing her to cough.

The giant uncoiled slightly to gain enough length for its head to come level with her, its scales sparkling brilliantly as it moved.

"All who enter this land are drawn here; it is the natural order of things. As for inside, it is the desire of all and the reward of the true, many have come to me claiming they are worthy of its embrace but too few prove they are ready to witness its glory."

It spoke with the upmost air of regal presence, tinged with the sadness of a long solitary life filled with nothing more than guarding its precious door.

Lisa blankly stared at the serpent with even worse confusion consuming her. She went to speak, but the creature cocked its head so quickly only a meagre gasp escaped her lips. The thing's gaze seemed to bore to the very depths of her mind. Its spell immobilized her, forced her to stand like a frightened deer as it slithered its way through her thoughts. Finally, it relinquished its dark tendrils and she stumbled back into its rough body.

"Hmmm, interesting..." it said heaving a long contemplative sigh, its antenna fluttering about. "Others minds have pleaded, begged and squabbled for me to let them within the moment they arrive. They have lusted for their chance for so long it blurs all other thought. But you... you are not like them. You seem hesitant, afraid... why?"

Lisa fought to keep her expression calm at the insult to her composure, forcing the urge to shout and rave in defence down with a hard swallow. What good would it do to argue with this thing? It could kill her in a second if it wanted. Furthermore, if she called it out as a liar, of whom she was still unsure, just because she hadn't seen any of the others this creature spoke of didn't mean they weren't real, no benefit to finding where she was or why she was here would become by arguing. Taking in a much more noticeable breath than what she wanted Lisa braved taking a step towards the things head.

"I-I'm not, afraid! If I were, wouldn't I have run?"

"A weaker human would, but no... You are proud; you feel the need to prove your distance from the common flock that traipse to me in troves. However, your mask is unneeded... I am not your enemy. I can help you, if you are willing."

"S-so can you tell me why I'm here?" Lisa cursed silently for her nervous tone.

The leviathan shook its head. "No, I am constricted to telling you only of where you are meant to go."

Lisa tapped her index finger to her lips letting her eyes wander back to the gate, to the other carvings of the odd, misshapen animals greeting her with the same familiarity. Still, she couldn't tell what they were.

"I'm meant to go in there? Why?"

"Yes, as are all who come to me. Why this is, I have never been given the knowledge." Lisa tried to speak but the thing quivered its many frills before continuing. "Nevertheless I, unfortunately, cannot allow you in. You are... not ready."

"But you said I was different," Lisa retorted, folding her arms across her chest, proud of her point. Luckily, it disregarded her rude tone lowering its head again level with her.

"Different does not mean ready..." it hissed back, "nevertheless, I believe you were lured here prematurely for another reason, a reason which will prove your worth and allow me to make an exception. You see... I am missing a crucial item that allows me to open the passage. A mischievous spirit, of whom I cannot even speak the name, has stolen it. Retrieve it for me and I shall allow you passage through the gate."

Lisa stood frozen with intrigue rather than fear, her unease of the leviathan's ferocious air dissolved into the misty depths of

6

ner racing mind. Why should it need her help? Couldn't it take back what was lost by its power alone? She looked again to the gate, the scent of pleasant flowers and the sounds of music drifted through the still air. It felt as if they pulled her, whispered in her ear to come closer, to give in to the promise of what lay beyond.

Shaking the thoughts away, she asked, "Why can't you get this thing?"

The creature suddenly freed her, uncoiling to its full length and turning back towards the gate.

"If you do not wish to help me, or yourself," it sighed, "then be gone..."

It slithered its way up the stone back to its static place encircling the gates center. Lisa turned to walk away. What responsibility was it of hers to get this thing, this key, back? Just as she stepped, the serpent spoke again.

"It is a shame no others will ever again enter the soft embrace of their destinies. Even you will be drawn back only to be rejected. But no matter, it is your choice to rob everyone of their purpose."

Lisa turned back to the thing now wrapped lovingly around its home, its head hung low from the center staring at her.

"If there're others here, why haven't I come across anyone else? Why've I been wandering for so long, alone? Where am I, *Snake*?"

Her fear of the monster vanished and she took a heated step forward. If it truly wanted to kill her, it would've done so already. What it said made no sense at all! She'd walked for hours, or days, or years, she could never remember truly how long it'd been, the beginning of her walk was so, fuzzy...

But she knew for a fact not one person had ever crossed her path!

7

The leviathan lowered its head so fast Lisa faltered back nearly tumbling to the ground, but she regained composure immediately.

"If so adamant you are to find answers, bring me my key. Only then will I be able to show you where you are."

Lisa gulped down the fear welling in her throat as the giant spoke. The serpent still hung close to the ground, eagerly awaiting her response, blowing about her long chestnut hair with every breath.

"Fine. I'll do what you want, but only for answers, not to get into that," she pointed to the hedge. The music still called, her fear swelling with every peak and valley of the eerie notes.

"Very well, but the two are one and the same..." it hissed, slightly annoyed at her firm tone. "Beyond this hedge, you will find the forest, home to a creature called a Nakki. A vile thing even I fear. It lives alongside the creatures of this place; they converge in those woods listening to its every word. Pay them no attention, their only goal is to make you lose your way; they do not deserve your trust. After this you will reach the cliffs, here, on an outcrop of land, will be a tree. The thief lives there, but you must be very careful with them. No matter what, never allow them to lead you across their bridge into the hollow center of the tree. Do so and risk being lost to its collection and become one of the dead stumps many bare branches."

Lisa hesitated before saying, "h-how will I know what this thing looks like?"

She looked past the hedge as if already able to see the forest through its rounding edge, but there was nothing aside from emerald grass and a wall of flowered bramble.

The leviathan ignored her inquiry, retracting its head back and closing its eyes. Lisa stood for a moment watching its tendrils flutter in rhythmic breath before shaking her head and stalking off following the edge of the totem.

8

Intrigued by what lay beyond the thick brush, and wondering, perhaps, if the serpent had been untruthful of its bounty, Lisa stopped away from the creature's sight, admiring the magnificent flowers adorning the wall. The music continued its call, telling her to come closer, inviting her to see what it held. Reaching out she pushed away the thicket of branches only to encounter yet another bundle of leaves and twigs beyond the hole. Lisa yanked on a branch determined to see what lay beyond. It snapped, stealing her balance and felling her face first into the bramble.

Hoisting herself from the tangled mass, she absently picked the leaves from her hair staring at the consolation in her hand. She chucked the severed branch back at its former body in a frustrated huff. Why couldn't she get through this hedge now? If all were "destined" to enter, why bar it off? Why make it so none could catch even a glimpse into its inner depths? And why was she brought here only to be turned away?

Leaving the frayed and broken promise of seeing into the hedge lying in the grass, Lisa gave one last glance to the gate before it vanished behind the bend of the hedge. She reached the other side of the column after what seemed like hours, and she stopped, frowning at the nothingness before her despite the leviathan's directions. How could she find this forest if everything but this hedge looked the same?

She whirled around to face the maze of branches again feeling a light tug on her dress. She put her hand to her chest in relief seeing the small, friendly fox before her. It gleefully approached pushing its head into her hand.

"Huh, where did you run off too?" she smiled scratching the fox's velvety ears.

The fox recoiled from her affection forcing the tip of its snout into her hand. A mass of warm, slimy wood dropped into her palm and Lisa brought the fragment of stick to her eyes. The branch of purple flowers, though covered in drool, was as perfectly beautiful as if still attached to its host.

"D-did you want me to keep this?"

The fox danced as it backed away, panting and baring a stupid grin.

"Well t-thank you..." she gave a false smile, feeling slightly a fool for accepting a present from a fox. The fox pulled on her dress again forcing her attention when she tried to walk away.

"What? I hardly think you know the way."

It danced again before running a few paces ahead of her away from the hedge. Lisa shrugged. Why should she be hesitant of such a small creature? It twitched its head back between her and the horizon with every step it took. Seeing no other choice Lisa followed the happy creature through the grass, leaving the pleasant music and fragrant flowers behind.

Chapter 2

It felt as if they'd traveled for days before the column seceded beyond the horizon. Throughout the trek, Lisa had great difficulty keeping alongside the fox as it bounded towards the steadily darkening line stretching before them. Though she couldn't make out individual trees, it was obvious the forest held a size equal, if not greater, to that of the plains. A bird not much different than an eagle, with a long flowing tail akin to a peafowl, occasionally coasted above the masses center. Her attempts to study it failed miserably, every time she tried it vanished, falling into the trees and leaving only blue sky in its wake. Perhaps it'd been a figment of her imagination? Anything could've been possible in this strange world, however, Lisa hardly doubted its reality, discerning it to be one of the spirits the leviathan warned. She could only begin to imagine what monsters lurked within the canopy. Horribly grotesque things with missing limbs, bloodied skulls and chests or even no chests or heads at all, floated into her mind. Shaking her head, she thrust the disturbing thoughts away into the mist.

"Perhaps some of the spirits will be gentle," Lisa said, feeling rather foolish for trying to speak to the fox prancing along without a care for anything else around it.

However, speaking the words herself, instead of hearing them from some foreign body, only heightened her misgivings. Lisa trusted the serpent to be truthful and expected all, or at least a vast majority, of these shadow creatures would be vicious. Nevertheless, she needed to continue, if not for the fact she seemed the only one able to help. No others had come to the gate. No one else even seemed to occupy this land but the leviathan and the gleeful little fox. All through her wonderings, she picked at the flowered branch, never daring to tear even a petal free. It held too beautiful an image to damage and, although still covered in slime, and probably worthless, she felt, for some reason, it held importance; remaining unable to place why.

The mist of her mind blocked everything...

Closer they came to the forest. Saplings littered the ground jutting out of the grass, proudly exclaiming their triumph of marring the perfect expanse of green. Soon the saplings grew into tall young trees reaching out with wide entangled branches ever more proudly. This change passed by completely unnoticed by Lisa, who, in her musings and absent fiddling, only had eyes for the ground. Her feet screamed for her to rest, the cool soil doing nothing to douse their burning any longer. But she couldn't stop. Every time she slowed her pace, or tried to catch the fox's attention, hopefully making it realize she needed rest, it'd simply ignore her and sprint on forcing her to continue tired and miserable.

Finally, after what seemed another hour, the fox stopped at a tree not much taller than her. Lisa hardly noticed it was even there, falling to the ground immediately massaging her feet.

"You don't care much for rest, do you?" she glared at the forests edge searching for the bird. However, it thoroughly eluded her sights, barred by the high canopy.

Though the fox happily welcomed the rest, as it too fell to the ground panting, it refused to sit still, continuing to shift its gaze around the field and towards the forest. Lisa felt its uneasiness radiate like the heat of the sun breaking free from a clouded sky. Though, she took comfort in knowing she wasn't the only one having misgivings of this strange land. She reached out to give the worried fox a reassuring pat, but sensing her movement, it moved away before looking back to her as it continued towards the trees. Begrudgingly, feeling the rest was hardly long enough, she followed.

Drawing farther and farther into the forest Lisa grew increasingly unnerved. Her heart beat fast and her hands developed an annoying tremor. This land was a stark contrast to the beauty of the fields. Trees, no more a sapling than she was, growing to monstrosities so high they forced her to crane her neck to see the tops, littered the landscape stealing the nutrients from the ground, disallowing the grass to grow. Light filtered through in full force, though it did nothing to warm the incredibly cold sea of trunks. Surprising, seeing as the trees here had no leaves to boast, as would a normal forest. Despite its intrigue, Lisa refused to give this strange phenomenon a second glance.

Misshapen, grotesque creatures, looking as if crossbreeds of birds and spiders, with long, green feathers and a hundred unblinking eyes, watched with a frightening intelligence upon their perches. Keeping her eyes to the fox they continued, their speed hampered from weaving around the massive trunks or avoiding the creatures many angry branches. Other animals scurried along the ground, some looking to be deformed deer bearing spikes on their backs, others having no limbs, not even faces, to speak of and hardly holding any semblance of shape. Before Lisa could get a good glimpse of any of these strange animals, they vanished only to reappear somewhere else just as suddenly. She shuddered and clutched her flowers close to her chest, shielding them from their hungry eyes.

She chanced a glance back towards the edge of the forest confident seeing the emerald grass would calm her rattled nerves. She frowned and her eyes fell to the dirt seeing they were so far gone into the woods no semblance of its edge ever existed. The sea of thick trunks obstructed her view completely. Lisa didn't even try to understand how they'd traveled so far in what seemed like only a few moments. The concept of how time worked in this land brought the mist back into her mind, along with its dull, throbbing headache.

Despite the eyes and spectral animals swirling around them Lisa flopped down exhausted, her back on a trunk rubbing her feet unable to walk any longer.

"We must discuss how often we rest!" she huffed to the fox, who, after noticing her befallen companion, tugged at her dress in useless persuasion. Its attempts to pull Lisa to her feet were short lived. The fox backed away from the tree she lay against, growling, baring its teeth and pawing like a rhino about to charge some foolish intruder of its territory.

"What's wrong?"

Lisa stood as quickly as she'd dropped sensing her little friend's unease. The fox took guard between her and the tree, growling incessantly. The tree itself stood an absolute oddity in the field of sky-high trunks and bare branches. Much shorter than the rest around it, its branches were thin, bearing long tropical leaves akin to the palm or cordyline species. The air around it lay suffocated with moisture holding in a curious bitter cold much too harsh for such a specimen.

Lisa's stomach flipped at the queer sight. Something in her head screamed for her to get away! Then, before she could move, the ground heaved violently, nearly knocking her over. The fox turned tail and ran full tilt through the mass of trees,

14

eaving only a flash of red as it disappeared. The many eyes watching them scattered and soon Lisa was alone. Steadying on another tree, she scrambled after the startled fox, but to no avail... It vanished before she took more than a step. The ground fell away replaced by a chasm viciously groping at her heels, trying to drag her down into the growing hole. Then the void stopped its advance allowing her to duck behind a trunk and slump to the ground panting uncontrollably. Everything went silent, the sweet smell of wet earth swirling through the air.

She peered around her hiding place, her eyes wide at what stood before her.

A magnificent pond overthrew a space a hundred feet across, a moss-covered stump stood alone in its center where the tropical tree had been. Its waters, despite bathed unabated by the light filtering through the branches above, were dark and cold. No plant life grew over its surface nor did anything swim within its depths. In spite of the ground's violent heaving the water stood as still as a frozen sheet.

Lisa braved approaching the new form, nervously playing with her branch. Her advance was short lived; the disturbing image before her holding her in place like shackles. The stumps bark turned a sickly brown before peeling away, greedily consumed by the inky surface below, revealing a distorted dark mass. The figure ebbed and flowed gentle as a trickling stream, expanding to a horribly misshapen form of a human, glaring at her with a faceless head. Lisa recoiled unable to breathe, placing a hand on her chest trying to contain her racing heart. The thing only stared, still as a statue, suspended upon the water of which it consisted.

"Hmm... have I seen your pretty form before?" it asked. Their voice gurgled and choked as if the water consuming it fought to drown them as they talked. Lisa backed off further as the creature floated towards the edge of the pool, moving not a limb. Though the leviathan had given no description, which she hardly could blame it, as even now she was lost for words on how, she knew this horrendous thing to be the Nakki of which they spoke.

"N-no, I-I've never been here before," she replied firmly yet unable to shake the feeling it was a lie. The creature seemed to nod its misshapen head, but its body flowed so much it was hard to tell.

"Of course, I must remember my place. A new face, but always the same purpose."

The Nakki bowed with its hands together in prayer like a priest asking forgiveness. Reaching the edge of the water it leaned out towards her groping at her hand clutching the branch, its legs unable to leave the confines on the pond. Lisa tried to get away, but a trunk behind her prevented her escape.

"Well, well, well. It seems that wretched serpent has convinced the sheep once more," it said.

Lisa scowled at the creature. "I'm not a sheep! And why should I trust you? You're no different!"

The Nakki sputtered inaudibly before straightening its posture and glaring at her with misshapen, angry eyes. "As are you. Heading out to do anything asked for a mere promise." Water flicked from where its lips would've been as it spoke.

"What do you mean?" Lisa took a cautious step forward but still held her stance well away from the pond.

"Oh, no insult meant, my dear," it reassured, "it is a... condition of your kind. Always ready to run headlong into the first task presented if even a chance of reward is present. I wonder if you ever stop to think, to ponder, if it is wise."

"I think I can decide for myself what's wise."

"Of course my dear, of course. I know you are smart and very," it parted its hands, gesturing to her as a whole. "Beautiful."

"And what do you know of me?"

"So you are not smart?" it asked, amused.

Lisa took a step forward. "No, I-I mean, uh, yes, I am!"

The Nakki let out a stifled drowned laugh. "Yes... yes... Very smart, and so rare to find holding such beauty."

"Enough compliments!"

"Ah, of course, you are too high of mind to fall prey to petty flattery. No, information is your crutch unfortunately, much like the majority of your kind," it said with coy intelligence, a distorted smile breaking over its ever-moving head.

"What kind of information?" Lisa asked, taking another step.

"Oh, things I could care less about... though, seeing as your guide has vanished, I know will hold different meaning to you."

"You know where I have to go, how?" she narrowed her eyes at the creature.

"Of course I know!" it snapped. Quickly it straightened its stature and recomposed its voice, "The times I have been so kind as to point the way tires me greatly. And, sadly, it's always squandered in the end..."

Lisa played furiously with her branch, the soft petals offering little to calm her. "What d'you mean? Others have tried to get that serpent's key back?"

"In a sense, yes, but unimportant. What is, is that I know."

"Then tell me!"

"Oh I shall... but first, tell *me*. If you believe me to be untrustworthy, why have you nearly stepped into my waters?"

Lisa leapt away as quick as her heart bounded to her throat, her bare toes mere inches from the pond.

The spirit cackled again holding its stomach as if the joy pained them.

"Why you— you're horrible!"

"And *you* have no idea what these waters can do! I am only trying to help."

"Then tell me where to go!" Lisa stomped her foot hoping to intimidate the spirit with her anger, yet, it only made her feel slightly childish. Nevertheless, she held her proud, demanding stance, brandishing the stick in defiance of the crashing wave of fear trying to drag her into the depths of panicked anxiety.

The Nakki bowed its sloshing head then outstretched its right arm to the side. "Continue on in that direction and find the tree soon enough. But you will be back, I know it..."

Lisa looked to where it pointed then around and up to the branches searching for the creatures still watching.

"Do not fear the animals; they will not touch what I tell them not to."

Then, as if it hadn't ever been there at all, it melted away into the pond, the waters staying immobile as a sheet of glass.

Lisa backed away, the image of the monster leaping up from the pond flashing before her eyes. However, after waiting what felt like hours, or minutes, she never could tell, the Nakki never arose. Thankful it was gone she turned the way it'd pointed, giving one last fleeting glance around for the fox. Nothing, not a flash of red nor the sound of startled whimpering broke through the sea of trunk and earth. She had no choice but to follow the spirit's misshapen limb. They may be a liar but where else could she go? The fox had run off, probably for good this time, and she could hardly trust the creatures perched above. Frowning, Lisa trudged forward all too happy to leave the pond behind.

Chapter 3

The Nakki's cackling echoed in Lisa's ears well after she'd left ts domain. She ran as fast as she could, not only so the reatures above or scampering around could have no chance to ttack, but to escape the horrid sound. Before she realized it, he trees had begun to disperse again as did the eyes watching er, waiting to strike the first moment of opportunity. None of hem pounced nor called nor made any movements what-oever. They merely watched in silence, just as the Nakki had aid, and despite the leviathan's warning. Soon she emerged rom the forest back into the emerald fields.

She hardly noticed the change. The curious event at the pond ingered in her mind only allowing her own worries to enter. Vhat had the Nakki meant? It seemed like it knew her, at least t assumed it did. Lisa pushed the unreasonable thought into the nists of her mind, refusing to question it any longer. The thing vas taunting her, trying to get in her head, trying to drag her nto its depths. It must be wrong, assuming her someone else. Iut who? No one else was here, or at least no one she'd met, nd she hardly believed she'd meet anyone now. Why didn't ny of the creatures try to mislead her as the serpent said they vould? Though horrid looking, they seemed only slightly listurbed and curious than angry that she'd entered the forest.

Not caring where she stopped Lisa flopped into the grass taking a well-deserved moment to assess her new surroundings. Having not noticed before she was pleasantly surprised at reaching the end of the dense thicket. However, her content vanished as quickly as it'd come seeing what stood before her.

The land ended abruptly, as if some giant had gouged away the ground with a shovel. Sparse outcroppings sat across the chasm with all but one holding anything of interest. A massive tree, much wider and taller than those of the forest, clung to the pillar with many thick, protruding roots. Its high branches were barren like the others, but it had a great many more to boast sitting upon a trunk so massive, yet so incredibly fragile, a massive hole ripping through the middle, they appeared as if perched on two thin table legs.

Lisa frowned at the sickly shell, pitying it for even attempting to cling to its sad existence. Standing she breathed deeply before braving to continue. If the condition of the tree was any indication of this mischievous spirits temperament, she had much more to fear than simple trickery and persuasion. Making her way towards the cliffs a bridge emerged out from behind the slight rise of the land stretching the gorge, connecting the trees lonely isle to everything else. The bridge itself looked positively ancient. Moss and grass grew along its ropes unabated, along with many boards having come loose from their bindings, plummeting into the abyss below.

Lisa braved peering over the cliffs edge only to have her stomach flip violently in protest. She recoiled overcome with disgust. Neither land nor ocean rested far below, only the dark empty space of nothing. She tried to quell her racing heart with fast shallow breaths. Her thoughts scurried away, frantic and distraught as she tried to put sense to the sight. Alas, she couldn't, and tried instead feebly forcing the thought of the abyss away altogether. However, the mass of forest behind only served to remind her of what unspeakable monster could lay within the hollow tree.

Shuddering Lisa refocused on the yawning gap between her and the tree. The expanse held a greater width than she'd initially thought and the bridge seemed fit to give way at the slightest touch. Grasping the ropes, she stood rocking back and forth trying to muster the courage to cross. She stared at the trees sickly appearance for long moments, wondering of exactly how it came to be in such a desperate state of being and if, perhaps, the creature within had any hand in its form. She thought fleetingly perhaps the spirit was reflective of the tree and that it held as disfiguring and feeble a form. The assumption gave her a false comfort, however, and the words of the serpent echoed in her mind just as she raised her foot to cross. Her eyes widened and she backed away from the bridge cursing at herself for her stupidity.

"How can I do this if I can't cross!?" she stomped her foot and clenched her fists so tight she nearly snapped her flowered branch in two. Her voice echoed across the still air like a rock clunking down an empty well.

The air fell deathly silent, even the music of the distant hedge disappeared. The bridge swayed violently in a ghostly gale. Lisa bound backwards tumbling into the grass as a shadow crept from the tree's wound, glaring at her with menacing red eyes. Then, it leapt from its lair streaking across the bridge with the speed of a pouncing cheetah. Lisa fell to the ground shielding her head as the thing froze before her, rising to a terrifying height. But it didn't attack. It merely stood high above her, silent as the air. Its presence forced her to shudder; her skin crawled as if she'd fallen into an anthill. The spectres scurried along her body content to sting and bite at any exposed flesh.

"A-are you the spirit that stole the leviathans' key?" Lisa asked before the eerie silence of the being drove her insane.

The shadow waited long moments before replying with a simple and heavy breathed, "Yes."

The word was but a whisper yet to Lisa it'd shouted across the chasm it protected. Its deep voice penetrated like a knife stabbing her heart just enough to force it to continue its frantic beating.

"You may stand," it said in a much calmer, albeit demanding, tone.

Lisa stood, her legs feeling as if turned to the very twigs supporting the trees many bare branches. She braved looking at the creature only to recoil once more. It held a form of a person garbed in long, flowing robes, yet its body was black as the void below the cliffs, broken only by glowing red eyes barely visible beneath its large cowl. It looked the part of every picture and painting of death himself, though, the thing carried no weapon. That hardly mattered. Lisa guessed it could dispatch any threat in a matter of seconds without aid of a scythe.

Taking in a deep, steadying breath, she went to speak, but the words died upon her lips as inaudible puffs of air.

The spirit raised its shadowed hand. "No need to explain to me, little one, I know your goal... I will help you complete it."

Lisa perked hearing it speak in such an understanding way, but her excitement at the promise of help died as fast as the words on her lips. Again, she steadied her breathing with great difficulty, asking simply, "Why?"

The shadow shrugged. "I am not like the Nakki or leviathan. I know your journey has been long indeed, and I aim to help all who enter this land leave it in the proper way."

"Is that why you stole the serpent's key?" Lisa accused. Her fear of the spirits form hadn't disappeared, but her aggravation at the constant lies grew close to outweighing it.

"To bring you here, my dear, to where you truly need to be," it spoke with the utmost compassion and understanding, resting its cold hand upon her shoulder.

Lies! All of it lies! The words echoed within the mists of her mind, yet, they seemed not to come from her thoughts, but a memory of words past said.

"I assure you, what I say are *not* lies. Your thoughts betray you, little one."

Lisa started and backed away from the shadow. "I won't believe anything you say. I know what you spirits are like, your friend in the forest made sure of that."

"They are hardly my ally, neither is that serpent!" the shadow shouted back, its eyes flaring with anger. "If not for the leviathan you would have left this place long ago!"

"Is that why you stole the key then?"

The shadow glided forward and extended its body like a cobra to its prey. "He is the one that steals from me!" it bellowed with the ferocity of a lions roar. Then, suddenly it calmed, its eyes, before flaring like a raging fire reverted to their dull glow. "I apologize. It is... painful to see one like you so easily fooled."

Lisa's glare at the creature faltered to the ground and she felt almost embarrassed. Who was she to judge the intentions of this spirit? She had no right to call it a liar nor monster nor thief from one unpleasant meeting of a completely different creature.

"Now, little one, I will give you the key if that is what you desire."

Lisa faltered back at the strange statement. "B-but if the snake is truly a liar, why—"

"However!" it interrupted, "you must do something for me, a trifle to one such as you," it added seeing her scowl. "Listen carefully, for I will not repeat. The Nakki values beauty above all else, becoming so obsessed it prevents the forests river to flow,

23

keeping the water for itself. You have seen the degenerative effect it has had on its form. Retrieve for me some of its waters and I will allow you what you seek."

Lisa shook her head in disbelief. "No, I-I won't speak to that monster again!"

"But you know how it lures its game... already resisted its temptations? No, you will, or you will never receive the answers promised to you time and time again." Pulling a dry, dishevelled leaf from within its black form, it placed it carefully in Lisa's hands then turned and headed back across the bridge.

"B-but how— I-if I touch the waters? Wait!"

It was too late. The shadow crossed the bridge as fast as it appeared, vanishing within the hollow tree. Lisa groaned putting her head to her hands, the rough edges of the leaf scratching her skin. How was she going to get water from that, thing, and why was this spirit so certain of her abilities? She tried to pull the answer from the mists, but nothing came through but the Nakki's gurgling voice. Its flowing limbs seemed to wrap around her, crawling like a demonic spider forcing her to shudder. She looked back to the forest hoping to see some sign of the fox.

Nothing.

Only the brown off the massive trees greeted her eyes. Straightening with hesitant bravery, she headed back into the woods. What use was there to sit and wait for something that would never come?

Chapter 4

Navigating the forest again, despite its simplicity, having only to walk in a straight line from where the bridge lay, was far from comfortable. At every rounding of a tree, the faceless deformities scurried away and the prying spidery eyes above lingered, content in watching their visitor from afar. Lisa attempted to close her mind to the enclosing horrors, but every time the image of the Nakki inches away from her face ready to drag her into the frigid depths of its pond flashed before her eyes. Any idea of how she'd manage to steal away any water from the spirit's pond thoroughly escaped her grasp. It was impossible, laughable to the extreme. The shadow didn't want to help her, it wanted her dead and this foolish errand only served to aid that goal! Yet, the longer she walked the more it didn't make sense.

It could easily kill, why not do it?...

Consumed by her musings Lisa drew ever closer to the pond. The air, elsewhere cold and dry, became like a misted breeze of the ocean. All the while, the other creatures hardly seemed inclined to do more than watch. Perhaps the leviathan was wrong about them? Lisa dismissed the possibility outright. The pressing matter of retrieving the water called her focus, disallowing her to question the snake's truthfulness further. Repeatedly her eyes wandered, searching for the fox, hoping it still followed, hoping, perhaps, it'd startle away the monsters. A pleasant sentiment, but far from the unfortunate reality. No flash of red caught her eye or streaked between the trunks, only the green-black of the deformed creatures scurrying about the forest. The fox had gone and it'd never come back. She sighed heavily; disheartened after spending what felt a day of hopeless searching, trudging along slowly as the time felt. What did it matter? Facing the Nakki was a fool's errand, disallowing any hope for survival.

Rounding one final, massive tree, Lisa unfortunately reached the pool. Everything following her dispersed in an instant leaving her alone in the clearing. The black water sat before her, the stump missing from its middle. She crept forwards making sure to stay well away from the exact edge.

"Hello?..."

Nothing in the grove moved.

"I know you're here Nakki, come out!" she shouted feigning bravery, but her voice shook as violently as her hand still clutching the flowered branch.

Still nothing stirred the waters. Had the Nakki gone? It couldn't have, she'd seen its inability to leave the confines of the pond. On the other hand, perhaps it'd displayed some form of pleasantry for their conversation. Nevertheless, she needed the water and she couldn't assume the spirits departure with a few feeble shouts.

"I won't ask again, please, I-I need to speak with you!" she shouted again, though, more to be heard than to project her own courage.

"The spirit has gone," a voice called out.

Lisa leapt away thinking the creature to be hovering beside her. Her eyes danced around the glade in panicked frenzy with nothing meeting them but the dark pond and bordering trees.

26

"W-where are you? Show yourself!"

"No need to be hostile to someone only here to help," the voice said.

Now Lisa could see where it was from. A beautiful bird the size of a peafowl, and with just as long a tail, sat high upon a branch overstretching the pond. Its stunning blue feathers nearly blended completely with the sky, leaving its eyes to appear as if floating within the sky itself. The illusion shattered as its wings broke its fragile confines and passed before the trunk of the tree in which it sat.

Lisa went to speak but the bird interrupted.

"You need to fetch water from the pool, do you not?" ruffling its crowned feathered head it shifted eagerly on the branch.

Lisa clenched her fist around the stick she held. These spirits needed to learn how to let one talk!

"Yes, what business is it of yours?" she leaned onto a tree folding her arms across her chest trying to feign the upmost look of boredom, but her fleeting eyes and grimaced face poorly exerted the same proud air.

"Such rude tones for one so young. One would think a prolonged stay in this land would teach you to treat us with more respect!" the bird snapped back. "And before you ask," it raised one large, elegant wing flashing its blood-red undercoat in pride. "We know how long everyone has been here, it is a sad knowledge, but one that serpent never lets us forget!"

Lisa's gaze fell back to the pool refusing to look at the liar above. The serpent was the only one that hadn't tried to kill her. Why should she trust any of what these spirits said about it?

Both refused to speak for long moments. The bird ruffled its feathers waiting for Lisa to move, to act as it wanted, but she refused. She only stared longingly at the pool waiting for the monster within to emerge.

It had to be there...

27

"What are you waiting for? Nakki has gone, that little friend of yours scared it away!" the bird said jolting Lisa out of the thrall in which the waters cast.

She scowled at the bird. "Hardly, the fox was terrified of that thing..."

"Quite true," the bird shrugged awkwardly. "but fear is never the true judge of one's abilities; any being can overcome it given time enough." It drifted down to a lower branch to come within a few feet of the pond. Its tail dipped into the water stirring it slightly. Lisa flinched at its sudden movement. "A perfect parallel to yourself it seems. So easily frightened by the smallest things..." a coy smile broke out across its beak, twisting it into a grotesque shape as if it'd been crushed.

"My fears are perfectly reasonable!" she retorted averting her eyes to the water refusing to look at the unsettling bend. "Giant serpents, ghosts, shape shifting water and talking birds would give anyone a fright!"

"Perhaps..." it shrugged again, ruffling its wings, "one often fears even what they have bested before. Hardly an excuse for you. Take the water, the Nakki won't harm such beauty!"

Lisa stared at the brittle leaf in her other hand, back to the pool, then to the leaf again, wondering...

Perhaps the bird was right. Nothing stirred the waters since she'd arrived, nothing arose when she'd called out, or when the birds' tail had touched its surface, and nothing lunged for her as she approached. Nothing stirred but her and the bird. It had to be true, didn't it? Despite her fears and despite the risks, she had to try. Getting the water remained the only obstacle in her quest for answers and nothing, not the bird nor the spirit's absence, would deter her.

Lisa crept to the edge of the water before crouching, extending the leaf outwards. The bird shifted eagerly sending silent ripples dancing towards her with every twitch of its tail.

28

feathers. About to dip the leaf into the dark pool Lisa paused staring with wide eyes at the bird. Its eyes were hungry and dark as the water, its feathers hued to that of the spirits limbs. She rose brandishing her stick at it.

"I won't fall for your lies!" she shouted stepping away from the pond's edge.

The bird's expression darkened for only a second before it smiled wide cracking its beak to the point of mutilation. It bellowed its gurgling laugh shaking its feathers clean from its body. They fell like a shower of crystal, dancing with every colour of the rainbow before falling mute within the black of the pond. The spirit fell to the water after them as if wanting to rescue them from their soggy fate. It rose slowly, taking obvious pride in its grand entrance, its flowing arms together in pray.

"I'm surprised it took you this long," its mouth distorted to a wobbling smirk.

Lisa held her branch out like a sword. "S-stay away! Just— just let me take what I need and leave!"

The Nakki drifted towards her, cackling. "But how can I stay away when you have brought such beauty into my woods?" they extended their arms out towards her brittle weapon, ready to pull it from her hands.

Lisa swiped at the monster forcing its recoil only for a moment. It continued on to the edge of the water where, once again, it halted. She backed away even more.

"Why are you all doing this to me? What've I done to deserve being tricked into my own death!?" she rubbed her lips with the back of her hand to stop their quivering.

The Nakki merely shrugged, its laughing fit finally gone, for which she was grateful.

"What did any of us do to come here, to be forced to stay in one spot forever, never allowed to have the beauty others guard!?" again, it outstretched its flowing hand to her, to the branch.

Lisa swung violently forcing it to recede to the center of the pond. It hung its head following a petal snapped free from its host in the heaving. The petal landed in the pond, pushing away the darkness of the water. For a moment, the waters became clear, rippling fast away from the intrusive body. The petal itself burst into the most beautifully vibrant blue-violet before sinking below the surface leaving the pond cold and black once more.

Lisa watched enthralled by the sudden change, a misshapen image leaping out from the depths of her misted mind. She reached out to hold fast to the form, to pull it from the fog, but it vanished faster than a startled rabbit. She stared unseeing trying desperately to bring the image back, but it was useless, she couldn't reach far enough and it slipped away. She glanced up feeling the flowing eyes of the Nakki.

"W-what... what happened?"

The spirit refused to answer, seeming completely content to watch her expression change from morbid curiosity to that of overwhelming confusion. Yet its gaze, however hard to tell where it lay with its flowing form, seemed not on her, instead resting on her weapon. She looked to the branch with wide, astonished eyes.

"I-is this what you've wanted?"

The spirit drew close reaching out towards the branch again. "From the moment I felt it enter my woods. Such beauty, and still so alive!..." it spoke in euphoric whispers, more to itself than to her.

"I-if I give this to you, w-will you allow me to take some of your water?" she asked, taking a step forward but keeping well out of reach.

The Nakki stayed silent.

Lisa waited a few moments more, but her foe remained enthralled by the branch. She waved her arm slowly with placid amusement as the spirit followed it with deformed, eager eyes.

"Fine. If you don't want it then I'll leave." she lowered her arm, checking a relieved sigh at her freedom from the strain. Turning on her heel, she started back towards the hedge, back towards the music. The gurgling, drowned cackle of the Nakki held her in place.

"A valiant try, but I know you cannot enter that wretched hedge without what the shadow holds, and you cannot do that without my water!" it hissed.

Lisa turned back but refused to respond. How did this creature know so much?

The Nakki shrugged again, a habit becoming incredibly irritating. "Leave the branch and I will allow you to fill your leaf."

Lisa stepped forward with the branch outstretched. The Nakki did the same, wrapping one flowing tendril carefully around the stick before tugging it free in one swift motion. Droplets of its body fell to the pond at its movement, but it hardly noticed, longingly staring at the flowers as it turned away gliding to the middle of the pond.

"Take what you need..."

Lisa bent down reaching out to the water. Her gaze never faltered from the spirit still ogling its beautiful prize. She plunged the leaf into the steely surface filling it to the brim. The shrivelled leaf immediately transformed from its sickly state into one full of life, gleaming with the same emerald as the field beyond the forest. She rose staring at her triumph, the same wonderment befalling her as the Nakki with its flowers. Pride befitting a narcissist welled up inside her forcing a sneer to break across her face.

"Thank you, spirit!"

The spirit didn't budge, still possessed by the branch.

Lisa didn't care. The need to get to the other spirit and the fear of how long the water would last quickly shattered her petrifaction. Her ability to keep the water in the leaf was incontestable, however, the amount of time she had with it was much less absolute. It could last forever or mere minutes, a fact made much more worrisome by times incredibly fickle behaviour in this land, content in remaining a complete mystery.

Lisa kept the water covered from the blasting light of the sky as she went to leave the grove. She looked around for the right way, thinking, perhaps, she'd made a trail to follow. Yet, she remained unable to find any clue of her past footing. The talk with the spirit had completely disoriented her. Nevertheless, she decided that, though the Nakki seemed docile now, she had to move away from its domain before it changed its mind. She trudged forward, unsure if the way was true.

The forest was silent, deathly silent, worse than it'd ever been before. No creatures rustled the branches above nor glared at her with their menacing eyes. The deformed, spiked shapes of the forest floor remained hidden within the sea's unseen depths. Lisa stopped her advance baffled by the stillness. Fear crept up to her like the worlds shadow consuming itself at dusk, slowly engrossing her. The uncomfortable touch of the phantom forced a tremor to shoot through her, jostling the leaf near to spilling. The music that was so present in the air vanished, consumed within the sea. The air grew frigid and the forest floor fogged like the mists swirling within her mind.

Everything was dead.

Then, a murmur drifted through from somewhere distant. It sounded nothing like the soft music of the hedge, stinging at her ears like wasps. The whispering chilled Lisa to the bone. Her heart pounded so hard it could've leapt from her chest and danced in the dirt. Again she looked to the treetops but there was nothing there. The sound grew louder, playfully dancing with knives in her ears, calling her closer, to allow them to lead her, to follow them to salvation. She followed, feverishly scanning for the mischievous culprits. The noise grew louder still, coming to a quiet whisper. She listened hard but the voices remained as incoherent as the murmured music of the hedge. Sure she'd come upon the assailants Lisa quickened her pace, but to no avail. The noise jumped away running from tree to tree away from her grasp, its enticing tones and mysterious words drawing her farther and farther into the depths of the forest.

Aggravated and determined to find its source she paid no heed to anything else around her, dismissing the glaring yellow eyes above, or the misshapen creatures encircling her along the ground as mere illusions. The voice echoed louder still, resonating as a petrified shout, but still the words were distorted, distant.

Then, a tug on her dress forced her halt. The voice fell silent, the many eyes and faceless bodies vanished in a second. Lisa blank feverishly trying to rid herself of her minds thickening fog. She'd gone so far into the forest nothing held any semblance of familiarity. Facing the creature pulling at her dress the pressure in her head tapered off, along with the frantic beating of her heart.

The fox panted before her, bouncing this way and that, before turning abruptly signalling her to follow. With a placid smile, Lisa trailed behind the animal without hesitation, glad of her guides return. Now she could present her worth to the snake.

Finally, she'd find out where she was.

Chapter 5

Lisa held much less enthusiasm of their destination as the fox apparently contained. The horrid red eyes of the shadow plagued her thoughts throughout the hike, tearing through the beacon that was her excitement of the fox's return. If she had any idea as to why it'd so suddenly returned, the feeling may have lasted longer, been able to withstand the looming fear of the spirit from breaking through, but she could only watch her guide weave through the forest with confusion. After a while, she gave up. Her gaze fell to the many faceless figures still skulking close by. Though the fox had scared them off to some degree, she couldn't be sure of the animals loyalty, knowing it capable of vanishing over some small fright, and unless the fox could speak, tell her its intentions, its presence would have to be answer enough.

Time seemed immobile, the sky forever holding its intense blue. Yet, to her, the sky could've been a deep shade of green and she'd have been none the wiser of its change. She felt as if a rain cloud had congregated above her, dampening her spirits with its incessant downpour. Staring at the fox's brilliant red fur offered little condolence, though, it was a much better altern-ative to seeing how close they'd come to the tree. She didn't need to look. The forests density had started to thin and the trees they did pass had shrunk considerably.

Soon the darker dirt of the forest exchanged once again for the emerald grass playfully tickling the bottoms of her feet. The creatures following retreated within the depths of the forest, whether out of fear of the shadow looming in the dishevelled tree across the chasm, or if they were unable to leave the boundaries of the wood, Lisa could never be sure. Notwithstanding their disappearance and the soft, cool grass once again quelling her burning feet, her spirits remained woefully distraught. Meeting the shadow again, however brief, remained a source of anxiety and she gritted her teeth at the coming displeasure.

Failing to notice, the cloud of misery looming so low it obstructed everything in her path, Lisa stepped on the fox's heel. If the animal had experienced any pain, it gave no indication. It'd halted mere steps from the bridge's rope posts, impassive as a statue. Lisa looked up, regretting her decision immediately at the grotesque sight of the half dead, waning stump across. Suppressing her urge to turn away, she stepped forward to call for the spirit.

Her bravery went unneeded as the fox blocked her path before making a quite terrible racket. Its shrill calls echoed through the air like an explosion bursting to its full ferocity not a foot in front of her. Lisa stared at the animal, utterly perplexed at how something so small could produce a call so violent.

The bridge swayed in the phantoms gale as it peered from within the hollow tree. The shadow emerged glaring at the intrusion, as if unsure for its own safety before barrelling across the bridge with the eagerness of a murderer closing in on their victim.

Lisa fell to the ground crossing her legs in a desperate attempt to hide she'd fallen of fear and not by choice. A splash of water touched her arm. She dared not avert her eyes from the ones speeding towards her. The fox, surprisingly, hadn't moved the entire ordeal. Lisa assumed it would've run off at the first sight of the horrid beast, as with the others, but it stayed, impassive as ever.

Leaving the bridge the shadow encroached upon them slowly, as if exhausted from the burst of energy. Lisa swore she heard it panting; however, it could've easily been the fox before her. The air went still. None dared make any motion. After what seemed hours, Lisa quivered bringing herself from the shadows enthralling eyes and offered the leaf. Without hesitation, it snatched it from her hands.

"I never doubted your abilities..."

"You have what you want; now give me what you stole!" She shouted back with renewed confidence, though by the last word her lips developed an unflattering tremble and her voice became a weak croak.

The shadow bowed its head. "I see you have not altered your thinking... unfortunate, but I shall honour our arrangement."

Having little contrast on its shadowed form the spirit looked as if it reached directly into its chest before withdrawing a golden medallion the size of its head. Lisa's eyes widened at the gorgeous pendent. A serpent lay carved on the medallion's circumference, shaped as if about to devour the sapphire set in its center. The shadow dropped the cold metal unceremoniously into her hands, the attached chain bunching up on top.

Lisa held the disk before her with some difficulty. Despite not holding much weight of any sense, it was much too big to hold comfortably with one hand. Hoisting herself up using the medallion as a crutch, she bowed low with regal thanks to the shadow. Even if it did try to send her to her death, it kept its promise and deserved her begrudged respect.

"Thank you, shadow."

It shrugged her affections off. "A hollow reward in return for what awaits you..."

Then, patting the fox on the head, the spirit turned towards its home. The fox sprinted past it and across the bridge with reckless abandon, easily skipping over the missing planks. Lisa staggered forwards calling for the animal, but her words went unheeded. Why was it leaving? Moreover, why did it trust this shadow?

"Wait, uh, shadow?" Lisa called as it drifted across the chasm.

The spirit turned back, its eyes dim and lifeless. "What is it, child?"

Lisa clenched her fists at the insinuation she was anything but an adult after what she'd been through. She took a deep shuddering breath and dismissed the comment with great effort.

"You know what's beyond the gate?"

"Yes," it said, its eyes flickering bright with intrigue, though, hardly having energy enough to remain so.

"C-could... could you tell me?"

Her heart fluttered at the chance of knowing if, by some twisted fate, she'd never have to trudge through that terrible forest again, never have to pass the Nakki, and never have to confront the leviathan, still unsure if it truly offered as grandiose a reward as it claimed. She only wanted this ordeal to end. The shadow had been just as, if not more, cordial than the serpent. What would truly be the cost of trusting it? Perhaps this shadow held more answers.

"No, that is forbidden..." it said, sounding thoroughly disheartened by the question.

Lisa's hopes fell placidly to the ground as the petal had to the pond.

No.

Always no! What secret did this world hold in such high status? Moreover, why did they all so adamantly keep it from her?

"However," it continued, "guidance is not... heed my words child, nothing good can come from going back to that horrid beast! Beyond the chasm is your rightful place, among the others. Allow me to see you safely off this land, I only wish your well-being." The shadow glided closer, the life in its eyes steadily returning.

Lies! All horrible Lies!

Lisa retreated from the monster ready to run, to flee with the amulet back to the one truly wanting her salvation. Despite the leviathan sending her on much the same quest as this shadow, it warned of their false promises, of their compulsion to tell only what she wanted to hear, allowing her reasonable defence against them. What other purpose would it have in doing so if not to help her? Why send her off if it hadn't felt her different, recognized her abilities, that she could handle its quest and bring the amulet back? The serpent was her only true friend. These other monsters wanted nothing but to torment her. Everything the shadow said were lies...

"Tell me, did the serpent ever explain why I stole the amulet?" the shadow asked breaking the silent air.

"W-well, n-no..." Lisa sheepishly retreated, but the spirit coiled its shadowed body fast around her preventing escape.

"Unsurprising," it breathed. The shadow took a slight pause as if collecting its thoughts. "I stole the amulet, the key as you call it, because of a cycle we are forced to continue. Again and again it is completed, reset and completed, whether it is you or another it matters little. It is a test of will, of intelligence and worth, as that serpent may have... forgotten to mention in any respect. At least I assume."

38

"So there was never any danger for me? I was meant to do this?" Lisa stared at it somewhat surprised, a distant figure in the mist of her mind yelling that she shouldn't be.

The shadow chuckled. "Oh no, there was indeed danger. The Nakki is not a spirit to be trifled with. It has very well trapped many before you and is a plague upon this land! It is only here because the serpent allows its existence! However, I was certain you'd complete my errand, like it has been so before."

Lisa's face contorted in confusion. How could this shadow have known she'd complete the tasks? It'd never met her before. Yet, neither had the Nakki nor the serpent, and both seemed all too familiar with her abilities. Had this happened before? She refuted the notion outright, it was only as they said, others completed it before her.

"So why bother if you all knew I'd succeed?" she asked point-edly.

The shadow drew in close, its narrowed eyes coming level with hers. "I never said anything about success!..."

"Then... then I'll go back to the snake, complete the test!"

The shadow withdrew its body regaining its full height. "Very well, but it will be most pitiful..." then, it suddenly turned towards the bridge floating lazily back to its home.

Lisa ground her teeth at the spirit's turned back. How could she figure out anything if they gave only riddles and more questions? The only thing she could count on to be certain was the fact that none of them, not the Nakki, not this shadow, not even the fox, were trustworthy. Traitorous animal! How could it have bounded across the bridge? Perhaps it wanted her to follow? No, that was unthinkable! She'd never enter that horrible tree! But how could she be so certain of the leviathan's words? She bowed her head closing her eyes, fighting the tears away.

She didn't know what to believe anymore...

Stomping the ground in frustration and at her inability for restraint, she chased after the shadow. She had to ask more, had to find out why they all seemed to know her despite never meeting them. She had to!

"Enough of the riddles!"

The shadow stopped shy of the bridge's posts, but didn't turn. Lisa paused a few moments trying to find the right question to ask through the thousands flickering like distant fires within the mist.

"Always so angry with no reason to be..." it said derailing her train of thought and leaving her with the most vacant of stares. "Though I guess it should be expected," it turned back angrily stalking towards her. "Searching for so long, yet always unsure of how far has been traveled. Always on the cusp of finding answers but denied. Yes I can see quite clearly why..." slowly the shadow circled around her. All the while it kept its gaze on its home. "Tell me, why do you think you have no memories of the time before this place? Why all seem to know and are eager to help, but always dangle the truth like a fruit out of reach? Why wandering this plain can feel exhausting while taking no time at all? Have you never wondered exactly why you have been sent here, or what you are truly meant to do?"

"W-well, I, that is, the serpent said I'd find out within the gate. That it's the fate of everyone here..." Lisa replied, hardly believing her words. She looked to the medallion sitting at her feet. She'd tried to hold it but its size made it impossible without both hands, and with both it became a nuisance.

"I have no doubt you will find the answers you seek, but perhaps the place in which all are drawn is not the place you discern to be right," still circling the shadows eyes never left the hollowed tree.

"I'm tired of these riddles! Please, tell me why I'm here, please..."

The shadow merely continued to circle and stare. "I have already told you! I gave you a task, as did the serpent, to open the gates. Retrieving water in a leaf was not a plan fished from the void below these cliffs. No, it has been completed time and time again."

"You've said this!"

"And still you do not listen!" it roared. "Have you not wondered what the water was for?"

Lisa shook her head, keeping her eyes away from the shadow, keeping it from seeing her tears...

"So naive yet so intelligent... I see you are missing a crucial piece to your outfit since last you arrived."

"What does that have to—"

"I wonder... when you gave the branch to the Nakki if you happened to notice a change in the water. Or, perhaps, the change in the leaf," finally it ceased it's circling withdrawing the shining green leaf to her downcast eyes, "when the water touched it's surface?..." it finished with a drawn out breath.

"I, I never thought—"

"Yes, pride often clouds ones abilities for reason... Regardless, I did not send you on a fool's errand for worthless water," the leaf disappeared into the spirits blackness again.

Lisa glanced between both the shadow and tree trying to re-member, trying to understand, and trying to search through the mist. Tears brought on by the sharp, stabbing headache fell haphazardly down her cheeks. The faint feeling of familiarity came to her, but nothing emerged from her fog. She didn't understand! Desperately she tried, feeling as if some spectral hand clutched hard at the back of her head, keeping everything just shy of her reach. Then she saw it. Instantly, she clutched the memory fast, pulling it free of its clouded prison. Her eyes widened and she faltered back steadying herself with the medallion.

41

"Now you see!"

If any smile could've been seen on the shadows face it would've stretched its entire head. "This tree was like the hedge, but, over time, and without the river, it has shrivelled and lost its former beauty. But with this..." it trailed off making its way towards the bridge again.

Lisa dropped the medallion's chain and followed the shadow.

"Now I have the power to share what has been haunting you for so long. You will know where you are," it said not halting its progress.

Could it really be this simple? She glanced back towards the forest feeling the many eyes within and those beyond still watching, waiting for her return. Did the leviathan truly promise lies? She passed the threshold of the bridge posts. It appeared smaller once on it and the ropes refused to slacken under her weight, tightening to that of immovable steel.

"But the key, w-why... why was I sent to retrieve it if it's worthless? Why did the music call me to the hedge? If I'm meant to come here then why wasn't I guided here first?" Lisa persisted.

The shadow slowed slightly. "What makes you believe you were not at least tugged in the right direction?"

This didn't make any sense!

The questions raced through her mind to the point of annoyance, but she dared not ask again. What use would it serve if it only resulted in more questions and riddles? So often the answer they were. Lisa slowed and the bridges boards creaked as she stopped. The roundabout answers and lies rested so heavy on her shoulders she felt unable to continue. So exhausting had they become. Once more, she attempted to penetrate the thick fog that consumed her head.

Useless...

Every semblance of memory flickered like a lighthouse in the distance, never staying long enough to be recognized. If this shadow truly wished to help her, to reveal what she craved, then why not tell her without all this trickery and deceit!

She looked up to the tree's unappealing branches wavering in an unfelt breeze, as if trying to signal her to turn and run. The same feeling of familiarity struck her like a rock to the head forcing her to check a gasp, fearing the shadow would hear.

The words of the serpent slithered into her mind refusing to leave, the sickly branches only aiding in the thought's power. Lisa averted her gaze only to be struck by the void below the cliffs, hollowing out her stomach to the same degree. It was a trick, just as the leviathan warned! The shadow only wanted to imprison her, to turn her to one of its grotesque sticks! She had to go back, had to leave this terrible place, had to return to the hedge, had to get away from this monster!

Silently she watched the shadow hover on across the bridge. It seemed to move so slowly compared to its furious entrance, as if exhausted from the previous effort. Lisa shook more violently every moment wanting to turn and flee, but she wouldn't dare with it so close. She waited and watched the shadow inch towards its tree. Finally, she felt it far enough an attempt could be made. Turning she crept away back towards the forest. The boards creaked horribly with her every step, but she kept moving, fearful of the shadow's response.

The shadow's voice tore through the still air like a knife through the skin.

"I see the serpent has yet another loyal sheep to keep in his pen!"

Lisa quickened her pace not daring to look back at the angry beast. Her attempt failed miserably and the shadow sped past her, expanding its form wide across the bridge blocking her path.

"I will not allow it!" it said, its eyes blazing like the heart of an uncontrollable fire.

Their glare burned through her chest searing her heart. She tried to look away, but they held her fast, as one stares at an animal torn apart by some vicious predator despite the horrible sight.

"Listen to me, girl, do not return to the serpent. Nothing good can come from it! Come with me, I can show you what you want!" it gestured a ghostly hand beyond. "Only I can give you the answers you crave!"

"Liar!"

Lisa ran straight through the shadow, its body chilling her as if she'd run through a waterfall. It shouted for her to come back, to accept her true destiny, but she refused its continued lies and trickery. Escaping the bridge, she dipped to grab the medallion before running into the forest. Just as she reached the trees, a tug on her dress froze her in place. She glanced back but didn't turn her body. The fox stood with her dress in its mouth, its eyes pleading for her to come back, to follow it across. Kicking its nose Lisa stumbled forward from the renewed freedom. She never looked back to the fox's yelping or the enraged agony of the shadow. She only looked forward, towards the hedge, towards the soft mumbling music, towards her freedom.

Chapter 6

Lisa stumbled through the forest barely holding to the medallion's chain, letting the large golden piece drag lazily behind her. How could the fox have wanted her to go with that monster? It had to be in league with the spirit and only guiding her there to trick from the beginning! Yet, why would it have deserted her at the pond, forcing her to trust the Nakki's directions alone? This she couldn't answer no matter how many times it ran through her misted thoughts.

It didn't make any sense...

The shrill screams of the shadow died away as soon as she'd entered the forest, allowing her respite enough to slow to a walk. Unfortunately, the calls of the faceless creatures wandering the forest floor and above in the branches replaced the agonized howling. The soft hum of music calling her to its embrace remained but a whisper, but it was enough. Lisa, whether founded in imagination or reality, found the tune had grown clearer since her ordeal with the shadow, with individual notes becoming audible for the first time. Still, the overall call was lost to her. Only the message beckoning her back remained discernible. She couldn't care less what the tune was, as long as she had a guide.

She approached the pond again unsurprised she'd made it so far having run the vast majority. The Nakki still lingered in the center holding its prize branch lovingly. Yet its eyes, or what Lisa could figure was its eyes, wasn't to the beauty it held, but to its returning visitor. Lisa glared back at its apparently smug demeanour.

"What're you staring at?" she shot, unafraid of the creatures tricks.

The Nakki took a deep, gurgling breath chuckling with immeasurable glee. "Watching the sheep prattle along back to its shepherd."

"And you're nothing but a parasite!" Lisa snapped, stopping her advance past the pond, her expression darkening.

After what she'd been through who were they to question her judgement? The Nakki glided across the water towards her. Lisa stood her ground as it leaned over the edge, its misshapen head stopping only inches from hers. It snickered, the gurgling sending a chill down her spine.

"Is this true bravery or arrogance now that you have that worthless coin?"

"This!" Lisa brandished the chain at the creature. The medallion lurched after it ramming her heel, to which she gave little care, "will give me the answers you all refused me!"

The spirit straightened away from her. "I gave more than enough answers, girl! You refused to listen! Not surprising, your pride of intelligence overshadows your humility."

Lisa glared at the creature with such anger it seemed as if it flinched. But when it bellowed its horrible laughter at her expression she let her eyes fall. Fed up with their arrogance she stalked away from the pond. The Nakki called to her again.

"What do you expect the serpent to give you in return for that trinket? Answers? Ha! There's only one who can give you what you want, and they are back from where you came!"

Lisa clenched her fists snorting like a bull before whirling around to face the spirit shouting, "Lies! Neither of you want to help me! You only want to drag me away and keep me like a trophy to gawk at! The only one that's truly promised me anything is the serpent and I'm taking this back to it!" She brandished the chain again before limping off through the maze of trees.

Lisa didn't dare look back; she knew what she'd see. She could hear the innate ramblings of the Nakki as it sputtered and fumed at her. What did she care? She didn't need its hollow promises and false rewards. She figured out the test and it aimed only to create doubt in her decision. Despite the leviathan promising the same, answers and the truth, they remained the only one uninterested in luring her into its trap at every turn, leaving her no reason to distrust them, having been shown time and again no other cared to aid her.

Even the fox had betrayed her...

Lisa continued at a brisk pace trying to focus on the soft music. The shrieking of the shadowed spirit and the cackling of the Nakki pounded incessantly in her ears. No matter how hard she tried, the horrid noises clung as a bur clings to ones clothes.

Reaching the edge of the forest the emerald grass gleefully filled every space between the saplings like a flooding river. She flopped to the ground exhausted, dropping the chain, rubbing her feet and staring off into nothing. Only the top of the massive hedge peeked over the horizon. Even at such a distance, it appeared to be holding up the sky with its thick, brambly walls.

Despite being unable to tell exactly how far she'd gone, or how much time had passed, there was no question of the ordeal the journey had been. Her feet screamed for rest all through the forest, a complaint she wholeheartedly refused. How could she have justified stopping? The many creatures always skulking close by, calling to entice her, along with being so close to her goal, forced her forward as if she were still following the traitorous fox.

She could already see the gate opening for her, the blast of bright light and swirling sounds of music that would surely greet her, already hear the serpent explaining away all her questions. She knew not where the images came from, but delighted in their promises all the same. She rose and continued towards the pillar.

Then, she halted, feeling a tug on her dress. She spun around and froze staring at the empty space behind her. She scowled at her dress thinking, perhaps, the medallion's chain snagged. Her expression only darkened as her dress continued its unabated flow. Perhaps the fox had come back to her only to vanish from fear of her anger. Unlikely, and even if it did, its traitorous actions were reason enough for her to refuse its desperate calls for forgiveness. Shaking the phantom feeling off, she continued towards the very real sound before her.

Finally, feeling as if she'd walked for years without rest, Lisa arrived at the sparkling quartz gate. The many branches, leaves and flowers of the hedge greeted her approach with invisible smiles reflective of their beauty. Lisa smiled along with them; though not back to them, that would be insane, but to making it back with nothing but sore feet and a bruised heel. The leviathan still encircled its center gracefully dangling its head. Standing before the gate, giving ample room for the serpent to come down, she called to it. Its eyes flared open at the obtrusive sound and, before she could take a step back to avoid its entanglement of scales and frills, it dropped trapping her within its speckled pen once more. The serpent's attention was immediately lost in the medallion's golden surface.

"Excellent, I had no doubts you could retrieve my amulet."

Lisa held the chain out to it. "Take it and tell my why I'm here!"

"Patience..." they hissed flexing the frills along its length. Using the tip of its tail, it snatched the amulet away hoisting it high above the ground to its eyes. "Child, you have definitely earned your reward with such loyalty!"

"Wait!" Lisa called up to the creature ogling its prize.

"What is the matter?" it asked in a subdued, almost impatient tone.

Lisa swallowed hard, forcing her heart back into her chest, her stomach feeling as if a fish swam gleefully within. Looking into the hollow black eyes of the creature, the image of the gate reflected within them, the painful stabbings obvious familiarity nearly overtook her nerve of asking, yet, still, she could discern nothing of the misshapen figures in her head. She'd made the right choice, hadn't she? She tried to push the doubts away but they rebutted with the same squeezing pains as at the bridge. She had to see for herself, know the reason those other spirits detested this serpent so much, and know why her mind called her away from the hedge. It could've been that the serpent was honest within a world of liars. Any oddity, whether safe or not, often gives the sensation of unease. However, now staring at the massive creature again, its long fangs, flowing antennae and frilled spines giving it a most menacing look, she began to wonder if the spirits had some truth to what they'd said.

"I-I want to know... why— why did the spirits warn me of trusting you?"

"Is not the answer obvious?" it replied, "using truth is a dismal way of attempting deceit or to lure prey into their never-ending traps."

Lisa thought hard of the words of the Nakki and discerned what the leviathan said to be true for it. But the shadow was different. It acted as if personally attacked by the hedge's guardian.

"The shadow said something about the tree being a gate. I-is that... is that true?"

"Yes and no..." the serpent sighed. It drew in close, eyeing her intently. "I wonder, when the shadow told you their sorrowful tale to coax you into their pathetic home, did they happen to mention that the tree, the true gate as it often refers, a pleasant little lie, was once a branch stolen from my hedge!?"

Lisa stared unseeing, lost in thought, murmuring. "So it is a gate..."

A flicker danced through her mind showing her once again at the tree but turning away before even crossing the bridge. She tried to focus on the image, unsure of how it could even be possible as there was no questioning her bravery in approaching the sad crossing. Her mind devoured it before she had a chance. Lisa snapped from her trance as the serpent spoke, its response completely lost to her. It didn't seem to notice her wonderings as it raised its head and continued.

"I rejoice at your return, and your ability to stave off their temptations," its eyes went once again to the amulet, "along with returning what is most important to me." Then it turned to the gate. "Now, you shall be rewarded with what was promised."

It released her from its scaly prison, allowing her to step towards the elaborately carved slab. It offered the amulet dangling precariously on its tail tip towards the gate, touching the coin's gem to the sparkling stone. A slit of light cracked through the slab as it split open, grinding horribly along an obsidian base and disappearing into the brambled column.

The pleasant smell of marigolds, roses, lavender and chamomile leaked from the widening fissure along with the soft sounds of violins, cellos, clarinets, oboes and harps. Finally, the tune of the music could be heard, but it wasn't anything she recognized. She mused it to be something one wanted playing alongside a very elegant or, perhaps more accurately, sombre occasion. As more of the gate vanished the light leaking from its yawning gap weakened, allowing her clarity upon the majesty it held.

A field of flowers danced in a warm westerly breeze. The sky held the same pale blue as above the emerald fields, save for the high, cottony clouds littering its expanse. In the distance a group of people sat in lines of chairs, the women dressed in elegant, vibrant coloured dresses, the men in dashing suits, staring at a wooden stage where others, dressed much the same, played the instruments with downcast expressions, as if wanting only to end their tune out of respect for the beauty surrounding them. Lisa gasped at the sight. A wide hopeful smile, long since gone from her normally firm expression, cracked her face. She knew it! She knew the others were horrid, blatant liars!

The serpent bowed its head in acceptance of her awe. "Thus is the reward of one who trusts. Go forth; take your place within the garden! All will be revealed once you enter."

"But why? You said that if I got the key back I'd be told everything!" she retorted, somewhat put off by the sight of others in more plain faced clothes mindlessly wandering the garden, picking flowers, or sitting and staring at the sky.

"And I have given you a way for that to happen," the leviathan nudged her towards the door with its tail.

She pointed to one man wandering with his hand to his forehead with sad, distressed eyes and dressed as if going to a wedding. "Will they be able to tell me where I am?"

The serpent did not look to the person in question, focusing solely on Lisa. "No, all that is required is for you to enter."

Lisa narrowed her eyes at the snake. This was far too strange, but how could she argue further, especially with how wondrous everything looked in the grove, unlike the shadow's tree or the

Nakki's frozen depths. Her mind made up she started for the entrance. A tug on her dress, much more savage than any before, forced her to stumble back just at the threshold. Once again, she looked to see nothing. Not even a snagged branch from the bramble held her.

"What is the matter?" the serpent asked, seeming quite annoyed with her frequent stops.

Lisa didn't answer. The same hand of familiarity gripped her with such violence she felt her head about to burst from the pressure. Still the fog refused to lift, but something within tried desperately to break free. Staring at the flowers as if they would give some hint, bring some inkling of recollection, her heart sunk to her stomach and her stomach fell even farther. A chill shot down her spine and her hands began to shake. Something was wrong, but she couldn't place it. The people sitting within the flowers or the ones placidly listening to the music, dabbing their eyes at the emotion the tune coaxed, looked as if they were old friends long forgotten, but none were recognizable. The man wandering the garden caused the feeling to squeeze at her head with such violence she nearly toppled into the grass.

The leviathan chucked. "I understand... you feel this familiar?"

Lisa groaned holding her head and shutting her eyes from the pain.

"Do not worry; it is normal to be nervous."

It pushed her over the obsidian on which the gate had stood, the warm summerlike air engulfing her like fire.

Finally, the pain released its oppressive hold and the fog lifted away dispersing into the warm air. The memories flooded back so fast she all but fainted from the rush. She saw herself finding the gate and speaking to the serpent, then again breaking the branch from the hedge and along to meeting the Nakki. Then, the cliffs flashed through and she stood speaking to the shadow, accepting the task of fetching the water. Again and again and

52

again, the memories flashed before her eyes. Every time ever more distorted and changed... The words were unrecognizable, not the ones she'd just experienced, her movements foreign. Then, the memories of repeatedly passing through the gate returned to her.

The music, before surreal and pleasant, changed becoming as if her own death march. The smell of the flowers fouled, degrading to that of rotted onions and meat forgotten for weeks in the open. The sky darkened and the air fell cold with the coming storm. Her eyes widened and her heart leapt to her throat. She whirled around to face the serpent eagerly awaiting its prey's reaction.

Lisa bolted for the gate forgetting so easily she'd tried it before and that it never worked. Still she had to escape, she had to make it to the shadow, tell it she was wrong and apologize for her arrogance! The serpent easily pushed her back with its tail and she doubled over into the cold, wet flowers.

"So many times you've repeated this cycle and each time I enjoy it even more," it sneered. "I really thought you figured it out, that the others had gotten to you, that I'd have to relinquish you to that shadow. Now I see they truly have no power!"

"Why are you doing this!? I-I did nothing wrong!" tears stung her eyes and she wiped them away not wanting to give the snake the satisfaction of seeing her distress, but to no avail.

"I know not what you did or why you have been punished... but take it in stride child, for this loop shall be your home until the shadow is trusted!"

The gates halves shuddered before crashing together loud as a thunderclap. Lisa leapt from the flowers to run at them hoping, somehow, to slip through their closing gap. It was too late... They shut fast and refused her repeated poundings against the cold stone. She bowed her head, tears flowing unabated down her cheeks. Why was this horrible being doing this to her? Why couldn't she have realized the shadow wanted only to help, screaming so blatantly for her not return! No, she had to be proud, be so sure of her first instincts, to prove nothing anyone said could change her mind!

No matter how wrong her assumptions were...

She wiped the tears away fruitlessly as new ones readily replaced them. She watched the garden slowly vanish, as she'd done so many times before. The stage and her family before it were gone, consumed by the encroaching white mist. Her friends sitting in the flowers and her father, sadly wandering the glade, soon followed, vanishing as if they never existed. She closed her eyes constricting her muscles waiting for the inevitable.

"I don't want to do it again..." she choked as the cold mist licked her hand.

The cloud engulfed her and the ground vanished beneath her sore feet. She fell, fast as a comet into the white nothingness. Then everything slipped away. The memories were gone. Once more, she felt the touch of cool earth and the tickling of grass.

Standing, she examined the endless expanse of emerald, ankle high grass. The ground felt as ice, a welcome relief for her travel worn feet. How far had she traveled? This she couldn't answer, but she knew she had to continue on towards the horizon, towards the sounds...

Made in the USA
San Bernardino, CA
09 June 2020